If Not for the
Calico
Cat

BY
MARY BLOUNT CHRISTIAN

ILLUSTRATED BY
SEBASTIÀ SERRA

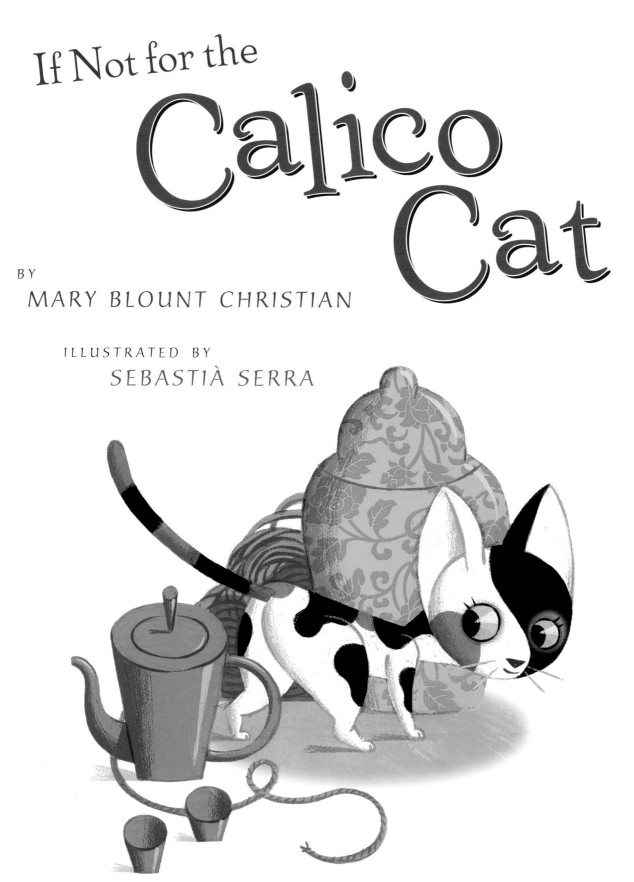

Dutton Children's Books

To Seth & Kaia,
with all my love—M.B.C.

To Sira, who loves cats
and the sea—S.S.

DUTTON CHILDREN'S BOOKS A division of Penguin Young Readers Group
Published by the Penguin Group • Penguin Group (USA) Inc., 375 Hudson Street,
New York, New York 10014, U.S.A. • Penguin Group (Canada), 90 Eglinton Avenue
East, Suite 700, Toronto, Ontario, Canada M4P 2Y3 (a division of Pearson Penguin
Canada Inc.) • Penguin Books Ltd, 80 Strand, London WC2R 0RL, England •
Penguin Ireland, 25 St Stephen's Green, Dublin 2, Ireland (a division of Penguin
Books Ltd) • Penguin Group (Australia), 250 Camberwell Road, Camberwell, Victoria
3124, Australia (a division of Pearson Australia Group Pty Ltd) • Penguin Books
India Pvt Ltd, 11 Community Centre, Panchsheel Park, New Delhi - 110 017, India •
Penguin Group (NZ), Cnr Airborne and Rosedale Roads, Albany, Auckland 1310,
New Zealand (a division of Pearson New Zealand Ltd) • Penguin Books (South
Africa) (Pty) Ltd, 24 Sturdee Avenue, Rosebank, Johannesburg 2196, South Africa •
Penguin Books Ltd, Registered Offices: 80 Strand, London WC2R 0RL, England

Library of Congress Cataloging-in-Publication Data

Christian, Mary Blount.
If not for the calico cat / Mary Blount Christian; illustrated by
Sebastià Serra.—1st ed.
    p. cm.
Summary: In Japan, the ship The Jade Lotus takes a calico cat
aboard for good luck, but the crew still runs into all kinds of trouble.
ISBN-13: 978-0-525-47779-2 (hardcover)
1. Calico cats—Juvenile fiction. [1. Calico cats—Fiction. 2. Cats—
Fiction. 3. Ships—Fiction. 4. Luck—Fiction. 5. Japan—Fiction.]
I. Serra, Sebastià, date, ill. II. Title.
PZ10.3.C43971f 2007
[E]—dc22   2006010445

Published in the United States by Dutton Children's Books,
a division of Penguin Young Readers Group
345 Hudson Street, New York, New York 10014
www.penguin.com/youngreaders

Designed by Irene Vandervoort

Manufactured in China   First Edition

10 9 8 7 6 5 4 3 2 1

any years ago, sailors believed that a calico cat aboard their sailing ships meant calm seas and safe ports. Perhaps some were, but others...

Long ago, when ships spread their sails like giant butterfly wings, people believed that the world was flat and no bigger than what they saw.

Which is why, two days after the crew of *The Jade Lotus* had watched *The Sea Pearl* sail away and disappear from sight, they were sure that it had slipped over the edge of the world and into a nest of sea serpents. But the crew also believed that a calico cat aboard their own ship would save them from the same fate.

As it happened, on that morning in long-ago Japan when *The Jade Lotus* was preparing to set sail, a calico cat was sunning herself on the wharf. She kept a wary eye on the sailors loading the ship. Finally, she hooded one green eye, then the other. Soon she slept soundly.

The sailors carried aboard shiny black boxes of polished jade stones, barrels of rice, and bags of green tea. They carried delicately painted bamboo fans and vases as fragile as eggshells. They carried bolts of slick, shiny silk the color of cherry blossoms.

Next came the ginger-jar-shaped cook with his coals and his porcelain stove and a pot as big and round as he. He had rice and rice flour and tangerine trees. He brought a fine fat milking cow and nine plump laying hens.

Then came the tailor with his scissors, needles, thread, and heavy, coarse cloth.

The captain strutted back and forth on the deck with the pride of an emperor, watching the stowing of each item.

Last came Hiro, the cabin boy, bearing the captain's compass and maps.

"Are we ready to lift anchor and set sail?" the captain asked his first mate.

"We have food to eat and food to sell. We have goods to sell and to trade," he replied. "We have everything we need except, alas, for a calico cat."

The crew folded their arms and refused to sail without a calico cat.

Hiro snatched a fish from the cook's galley and scampered onto the wharf. "Meow, meow, meow!"

The calico cat's nose twitched. Her slivered eyes grew wide, like twin moons. *Mrrrrrrt?* She licked her whiskers in sweet anticipation of a meal she didn't have to scrounge for herself.

Too quickly, Hiro reached to grab her.

She arched her back. *Pfffffft!* she scolded. But the fish's smell drifted toward her. Cautiously she crept closer, her nose quivering. Warily she stretched to touch the fish with one paw. But before she could say *Pfffffffft!,* Hiro grabbed her.

She hissed and scratched as Hiro carried her aboard *The Jade Lotus.*

Satisfied, the sailors unfurled the sails. The ship lurched forward. The captain turned the ship's arrow-sharp bow toward that place where the sky and the sea met.

The calico cat scampered about the ship. Everywhere she looked there was water. Her beloved wharf was no more than a thin gray line.

The sailors sailed. The cook cooked. The tailor mended. The captain peered at his maps. The calico cat sulked.

When *The Jade Lotus* had been at sea two weeks and a day, the calico cat wandered into the ship's galley. Pitty-pat— she leaped atop the barrel of rice flour. It felt like the soft white sand near her beloved wharf. *Rrrrrrrr.*

"Aiyeee!" the cook yelled and chased her away.

The calico cat ran into the captain's cabin and leaped onto his desk. *Pat, pat, pitty-pat.* She ran across his maps, leaving floury paw prints.

Zap! The captain swatted her away with the sleeve of his kimono.

Pfffffft! Was there no place made for a cat? She found some shade beneath a billowing sail, and there she curled into a ball to sleep. But something brushed across her. Her eyes snapped open. A dangling rope moved across her body with each dip and rise of the ship. Angrily, she swiped at it. The sail shifted ever so slightly. The ship turned its bow ever so slightly, too.

Meanwhile, the captain studied his maps. "Hmmm," he said. "I never noticed these paw-shaped islands before. Tell the wheelman to turn the ship ten degrees northward," he told Hiro.

The *Jade Lotus* sailed for weeks. The water grew colder and choppier. By day the captain frowned at his maps. By night he scowled at the stars. "The sky is all wrong," he told Hiro. "Nothing is where it should be."

On the evening of the third full moon at sea, Hiro brought a pot of steaming hot tea to the captain. "What if we are sailing too near the edge of the world?" the captain said.

Hiro set the tea on the captain's desk. "If we were near the edge of the world, would the air not be hot from serpents' breath? Yet we are chilled," he told the captain. "The good fortune of the calico cat is with us," Hiro reminded him.

When the captain went on deck, the calico cat cautiously leaped onto the desk, knocking over a cup of tea. Like a river, the tea rolled over the maps and onto the floor, carrying with it the paw-shaped islands.

The sea grew dark and foreboding. It slid across the deck, carrying with it buckets and lanterns and coils of rope. Angry indigo clouds swirled and puffed like dragons against a gray sky. The sails ripped from their masts. The tailor couldn't finish mending one sail before another ripped apart. The deck became slick and slippery with a thin layer of ice.

The cat found a warm spot beneath
the cook's stove and slept cozily, until
the cook stepped on her tail.

She fled to the deck. Sailors' feet skittered here and there. Was there no place where a cat could be safe? She saw the milk cow standing inside her fence, straddle-legged, swaying with the motion of the ship. The calico cat sprang onto the cow's back. The ship pitched, and the cat dug her sharp claws into the cow's hide.

Startled by the pain from the needlelike claws, the cow lowered her head and kicked her hind legs in protest. The pen tumbled down around her. She kicked the bamboo cage of the nine plump laying hens.

Crash! went the cage. Awwwwk! Hens flapped in every direction. One fluttered into a tangerine tree.

The tree trembled, and tangerines tumbled onto the deck like marbles from a sack. They thumped against the boxes, bumped into the barrels, and slid under the sailors' feet.

Arrrrk! one plump hen complained. She flapped to the top of the tailor's head, where she clung tightly.

"Aiyeee!" the tailor yelled in surprise, and flung his hand up. His needle struck the captain, who let go of the ship's tiller.

With no one at its tiller, the ship sailed in ever-widening circles until it thudded *ka-whump!* into a floating island of ice. The ship's hull crumpled like rice paper and swallowed seawater like a thirsty dog.

"Abandon ship!" the captain shouted. Hiro grabbed the calico cat. Barrels of rice, bolts of fine silk the color of cherry blossoms, delicately painted bamboo fans, and vases as fragile as eggshells slid into the icy sea to bob like fishing corks.

First came the sailors. Then came the ginger-jar-shaped cook with his sloshing soup pot. Next came the tailor with his mending thread and needles. Then came nine plump laying hens, their feathers wet and ruffled. Afterward, the fine milk cow with a mournful *moo*. Hiro, still clutching the calico cat, crawled onto the icy float. Last came the captain.

The *Jade Lotus* gurgled. It belched. Then it was gone.

The seawater seeped into the bobbing barrels and swelled the rice. The barrels exploded with a loud pop. Soft, fluffy rice flew into the air and fluttered down like flurries of snow.

And what did they see through the rice flurries but *The Sea Pearl*! Peering down at them from its railing were the moon eyes of a calico cat. *Mrrrrrt?* it said. It switched its tail from side to side. The crew of *The Sea Pearl* reached out eager hands to pull those from *The Jade Lotus* aboard.

Mrrrrrt! their own calico cat answered as she scrambled aboard.

When all of them were safe and dry, Hiro took a pot of ginseng tea to his captain. "We were most fortunate," Hiro said as he plumped the captain's pillow.

The captain glumly rested on the bed. "I have lost all my trade goods. My beautiful ship is at the bottom of the sea. What is fortunate about that?"

"Oh," Hiro replied, "just think what might have happened if not for the calico cat."

The captain moaned and shook his head. "Indeed, if not for that cat. Just think!"

At the foot of the captain's bed came a soft, contented *mrrrr*. Ah, at last, the perfect place for a cat!